the Jenius

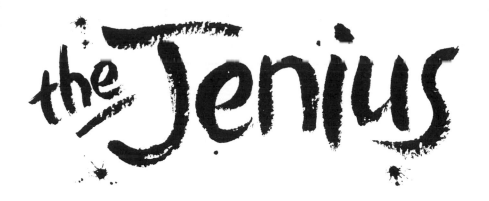

the Jenius

DICK KING-SMITH

ILLUSTRATED BY
PETER FIRMIN

PUFFIN BOOKS

"If I was the Queen," Judy said, "I wouldn't have corgis."

"What sort of dogs would you have, Judy?" said her teacher.

The class were talking about pets and which were their favourites.

"I wouldn't have dogs at all."

"What would you keep then," said Judy's teacher, "if you were the Queen?"

"Guinea-pigs," said Judy.

Everybody burst out laughing and Judy went very red.

"They're my favourite animals," she said

defiantly. "If I was the Queen I'd keep lots of them."

"In hutches, you mean?"

"No. In Buckingham Palace."

"But Judy," said her teacher, "wouldn't it look rather odd if someone very important came to call, like, say, the President of the United States of America, and the Queen, I mean you, said 'Do take a seat, Mr President', and there was a guinea-pig lying in the armchair?"

"And there'd be messes all over the carpet," someone said.

"And the President would step in them," said someone else.

Everybody giggled.

"My guinea-pigs would be house-trained," muttered Judy, close to tears.

"Palace-trained, you mean," said a voice, and now there was so much sniggering that the teacher said "That's enough, children."

She put her hand on Judy's shoulder and said "It's a nice idea, but even if you were the Queen you wouldn't be able to train a guinea-pig like you can train a dog. Only

cortain animals are intelligent enough to
be taught things by humans, and I'm
afraid guinea-pigs are not among them.
They're dear little creatures, Judy, but
they haven't got a lot of brains."

"You *have* got a lot of brains," said Judy.

As always, she had run down to the shed
at the bottom of the garden the moment
she arrived home from school, to see her
own two guinea-pigs. One was a reddish
rough-haired boar called Joe and the other
was a smooth-coated white sow by the
name of Molly. Judy had had them ever
since her sixth birthday, nearly two years

ago now, and they were very dear to her. Her only regret was that, surprisingly, they had never had babies.

"You *have* got brains," she said, "I'm sure of it. It's just that no one's ever taught you to use them. Now, if I'd had you when you were tiny, I bet I could have taught you lots of things. If only you'd had children of your own. I'd have chosen one of them and kept it and really trained it, from a very early age. I bet I could have done."

As usual, the guinea-pigs responded to the sound of her voice by beginning a little conversation of their own. First Joe made a grumbling sort of chatter (which meant 'Molly, you're as lovely now as the day I first set eyes on you'), and then Molly gave a short shy squeak (which meant 'Oh Joe, you say the nicest things!').

Then they both squealed long and loudly at Judy. She knew what that noise meant. They were telling her to cut the cackle and dish up the grub.

"Greedy old things," she said, and she picked up the white one, Molly.

"Molly!" said Judy. "You look awfully fat. Whatever's the matter with you?"

Molly didn't reply. Joe grunted in a self-satisfied sort of way.

"I'll have to put you on a diet," said Judy firmly, "starting tomorrow."

But next morning, when she went to feed the guinea-pigs, the white one, she found, looked quite different.

"Molly!" said Judy. "You look awfully
thin. Whatever's the matter with you?"

This time they both answered, Molly
with a series of small happy squeaks and
Joe with a low proud grumble, as they
moved aside to show what had happened.
There between them was a single, very
large, baby guinea-pig, the child of their
old age. It was partly white and smooth
like its mother and partly red and rough
like its father.

To Judy's delight it stumbled forward on
feet that seemed three sizes too big, until it
bumped the wire of the hutch-front with its
huge head. Its eyes were very bright and

seemed to shine with intelligence. Then it spoke a single word in guinea-pig language. Anyone could have told it meant "Hullo!"

"Oh!" said Judy. "Aren't you beautiful!"

"He gets it from his mother," chattered Joe in the background.

"And aren't you brainy!"

"He takes after his dad," squeaked Molly.

Judy stared into the baby's eyes.

"You," she said, "are going to be the best-trained, most brilliant guinea-pig in the whole world. And you're going to start lessons right away. Now then. Sit!"

Of course, when you're only a few hours old, standing can be tiring, but was that the reason why Joe and Molly's son immediately sat down?

✳   ✳   ✳

That night, before she went to bed, Judy wrote the great news in her diary. She was very faithful about putting something in it every day, even if sometimes it was only a bit about the weather. But that Joe and Molly should have had a baby — that was great news and deserved a lot of space.

JUDY'S DAIRY. PRIVIT.

JUNE 10th: Great surprise! Molly had a baby! Found him first thing this morning and I am going to train him. Alreddy he sits when he is told. He is briliant. He is mostly white like Molly but he has a sort of main like a horse running all down his back and that is redish like Joe.

∴ I asked Dad what you call some one who is really briliant and he said 'A jenius.' Why?' and I said 'because that is what I'm going to call my new baby guinea-pig' and he laughed but I said 'You just wait. One day the World will know June 10th is the birthday of Jenius.'

June 10th was in fact a very good time for
Jenius to have been born, because it meant
that he was around six weeks old by the
time the long summer holidays began. Now
his trainer would be able to concentrate
on him without the interruption
of school.

During those six weeks Jenius had
grown amazingly. All baby guinea-pigs do,
of course, but he had benefited
particularly, first from being an only child
and so getting all his mother's milk, and
secondly from Judy's spoiling.

Ordinary guinea-pigs, for example,
might get the occasional piece of
stale bread. Jenius got regular
digestive biscuits.

So that Judy's diary, which had contained daily reports of the progress of the wonder child, read…

JULY 22nd: Begining of Summer Hollidays. Today I took Jenius away from his parents and put him in the spare hutch, he is reddy to start his training, he is alreddy half as big as Joe, he is alreddy very good at sitting when he is told because that is what I have consentrated on but now I am going to teach him 'Come' and 'Stay' and 'Down'. Joe and Molly don't seem to miss him.

Joe and Molly were actually quite glad to see the back of Jenius.

Molly was thankful not to be nagged for the milk she no longer had, and Joe, though at first proud of the obvious cleverness of his son, was growing tired of being patronised.

"Thinks he knows it all," he grumbled to Molly, "with his 'No, Dad, you've got that wrong' or 'No, Dad, you don't understand'. I said to him 'When you've been around us long as I have, my boy, then maybe you'll know a thing or two'."

"Quite right, dear," murmured Molly. "What did he say then?"

"He said 'When I've been around as long as you have I'll know hundreds of things'. Cheeky young devil!"

"Ah well," sighed Molly. "He's only young, Joe dear. We're all of us only young once."

"Molly," said Joe. "You're as lovely now as the day I first set eyes on you."

"Oh Joe," said Molly, "you say the nicest things!"

"Mum! Mum!" cried Judy, bursting in from

the garden with Jenius in her arms. "Guess what!"

"Not now, Judy," said her mother. "I haven't got time for guessing games this morning what with the washing and the ironing and I've got a lot of cooking to do never mind the housework. Off you run and play, out of my way, please."

"But Mum, Jenius comes when he's told!"

"Very clever, dear. Now you go when you're told, there's a good girl."

"She just didn't listen to what I was saying," said Judy as she sat on the lawn with Jenius on her lap.

Jenius replied with a small sympathetic whistle which meant, Judy felt sure, "Grown-ups are hopeless, aren't they? I expect it'll be just the same when you tell your dad."

And it was.

"Comes when you call him, does he?"
said her father from behind his evening
paper.

"Yes, Dad! Honest! Don't you want to
see?"

"Not now, pet, I've had a long day. You go
and teach your precious genius something
else."

"What like?"

"Oh, reading, writing, some sums. Start
with the two-times table — guinea-pigs
are good at multiplying. Buzz off now,
there's a good girl."

JULY 23rd: I think Mum and Dad
grew up in Vicktorian days, they
think that childeren should be seen
and not herd. I am not going to bother
to tell them anything about Jenius any
more but only write about him in this
dairy so that the World will know
how clever he is when I am ~~DED~~
Dead and Gone.

In the darkness of the garden shed Jenius squeaked from the spare hutch "Mum! Dad! Guess what!"

"Not now, dear," said Molly.

"But guess what I learned today!"

"Hundreds of things, I imagine," said Joe sourly.

"No, only one. I learned to come when called."

"Well, now learn to shut up," said Joe. "It's late."

"Your father's right, dear," said Molly. "Go to sleep now, there's a good boy."

Throughout those fine sunny summer holidays the flowering of Jenius came into full bloom.

Judy was the ideal trainer, patient and hard-working, and her new pet was the perfect pupil. He enjoyed his lessons, he learned quickly, and what he had learned he seldom forgot. They made a great team.

AUGUST 15 th : Here is a list of the things
I have trained Jenius to do :—
1. COME.   2. SIT.

3. STAY.   4. DOWN.

5. WALK ON A LEED.
(I do not make him
walk to heal because I might tred on him
so he walks a little bit in front of me.)
   Before the end of the Hollidays I am
going to teach him three speshial tricks;
(A) 'Speak'. That is to make
       a noise when he is told (I suppose
       I should call this 'SQUEAK'.
(B) 'Trust'. That is
       balancing a bit of
       biskit on his nose.
(C) 'Die For Your Country'.
       He has to lie quite still with his
       eyes shut pretending to be Dead.
If I can teach him all these things
before the begining of Term I will take
him to school and show them all just
what a <u>Jenius</u> can do.

Every day trainer and trainee worked at
their lessons. And every night Jenius kept
his aged parents awake long after their
proper bedtime, telling them all the clever
things he had learned to do. He had
become, it must be said, a bit of a bighead.

Molly, who was rather vague by nature,
did not listen very carefully to her son's
boasting, and only yawned and said "Very
nice, dear," now and then, but Joe became
irritable.

"You must be the most brilliant guinea-
pig there has ever been," he would say

sourly, but this did not improve matters,
for Jenius always replied "I am, Dad, I am"
in a voice so smug that it made Joe's teeth
chatter with rage.

"Cocky young blighter," he would mutter
to Molly. "One of these fine days he's going
to be too clever for his own good."

And Joe was right. One of those fine days
came quite soon.

Jenius had woken early. He looked out of
the shed door (which Judy always left open
on warm nights) and saw a number of

attractive things outside in the garden.
There were lettuces and cabbages and the
feathery tops of carrots and the shiny dark
leaves of beetroot — all very appealing to a
growing lad. Why wait to be fed, he
thought. I'll feed myself.

"Mum!" he called. "I'm going for a walk."

Molly came to the front of her hutch and
looked across the shed.

"Don't be silly, dear," she said. "You
can't."

Joe joined her.

"In case you hadn't noticed," he said
sarcastically, "there's a door on the front of
your hutch."

"Dad," said Jenius in a patient tone of
voice, "doors are meant to be opened."

"I know that, boy. By humans. From
outside. Not by us from inside. If you can
open the door of that hutch from inside, I'll
eat my hayrack."

Each hutch had an outward-opening
wire door, kept shut by a two-inch turn

button, a simple device capable of keeping
prisoner every guinea-pig that had ever
lived. Except the Jenius.

Sitting up on his bottom as he had
learned, he reached a forepaw through the
wire mesh and turned the button
vertically. The door swung open, and down
he hopped.

He paused at the entrance to the shed.

"Dad," he called, "don't forget to eat your
hayrack," and off he trotted.

What happened next was recorded by a short dramatic entry in the diary.

> **AUGUST 26 th:** Jenius got out and was nearly killed! I am keeping the door of the shed shut in case he esscapes again.

Jenius was sitting happily in the sunlit vegetable garden, nibbling a tender young lettuce plant and thinking what a clever chap he was, when he heard his name called. He looked up and saw Judy leaning out of her bedroom window.

"Whatever are you doing out there?" she said, and since Jenius made no reply, she issued two commands.

"Sit!" she said, and "Stay!"

Jenius obediently sat down, quite content to remain where he was, in easy reach of such nice food.

Judy was just turning away from her window when to her horror she saw the big tabby tom cat from next door drop down from the dividing wall. Slowly, stealthily, he began to stalk the lettuce-eater.

Judy thought frantically. If she left Jenius dutifully sitting and staying, he was a goner. If she called "Come!" the cat would surely overtake him before she could get downstairs.

There was only one thing to be done, only one order she could give that might perhaps puzzle the hunter for long enough for her to rush to the rescue.

"Jenius!" she yelled in the fiercest most commanding voice she could manage. "Die For Your Country!"

Jenius, accustomed as he now was to receiving odd orders at odd times, instantly collapsed flat on his side. He stopped chewing his mouthful of lettuce, he closed his eyes, and even the rise and fall of his ribs seemed to have stopped, so lightly did he breathe. He lay, slack and still, looking every inch as he was meant to look. Dead.

"Dead!" said a voice in his ear suddenly.

Jenius' blood ran cold at the sound of this harsh cruel voice, at the smell of hot rank breath, at the tickle of long whiskers as something sniffed him all over.

"Pity," said the cat. "Could have had a bit of sport if you'd been alive. Ah well, a dead tail-less rat is better than no rat at all," and with that he began to lick at his victim's head.

Try as he would, Jenius could not keep his upper eye shut. Under the rasp of the cat's tongue the eyelid was pulled back, and he saw, only inches away, a nightmare face. A merciless face it was, with glowing yellow eyes and a wide mouth filled with sharp white teeth. Despite himself, Jenius gave a little shudder.

"Aha!" hissed the cat. "Not dead after all!" and he opened that wide mouth. But before he could close it again, a clod of earth hit him on the ear and a furious voice yelled "Scat!" as Judy came galloping to the rescue. She knelt among the lettuce plants beside the motionless figure of the Jenius.

"It's all right!" she cried. "He's gone. You can get up now."

As always she used the system of praise-and-reward by which she had trained him.

"*What* a good boy!" she said, and from the pocket of her dungarees she took one of his favourite digestive biscuits and broke off a bit.

Jenius did not move. Now it was Judy's blood that ran cold. Fearfully she lifted the limp body. There was no mark upon it, no blood to be seen. Could he have died of shock?

"Jenius!" cried Judy frantically in his ear. "Speak to me. Speak!"

Even though he had fainted with fear at the sheer horror of the experience, the sound of a familiar command was enough to bring him to his senses.

Feebly, through that unchewed mouthful of lettuce, the Jenius obediently uttered a single strangled squeak.

It was a much reduced Jenius that Judy replaced in his hutch, and when Molly asked "Had a nice walk, dear?" he did not answer.

"What's the matter, son?" said Joe. "Cat got your tongue?"

AUGUST 26th: Jenius escaped a ~~the~~ horribel Death!

Jenius had no intention of escaping again. He had had the fright of his life and, for a little while, his parents were spared their son's bragging and they could enjoy some early nights.

But before long he forgot, and his natural cockiness returned, particularly when he at last mastered the most difficult trick of the exercises that Judy set him. This was the ending to the trick called "Trust".

Not only had he to balance a piece of biscuit on the end of his nose, but then, when Judy said "Paid for!", he had to toss up the food with a jerk of his head and catch it in his mouth.

Jenius never tired of telling his mother and father how easy this trick was.

"Mind you," he said, "I'm the only guinea-pig in the world who can do it, I'm sure of that."

"Very nice, dear," said Molly absently.

"Pride," muttered Joe darkly, "comes before a fall."

SEPTEMBER 3rd: Jenius has quite recovered. Tomorrow is the last day of the Hollidays and I am going to give him a Test. I am going ~~the~~ to make him do all the things he has been taut and he has got to do them correcktly and I shall give him marks for his performants in each one.

SEPTEMBER 4th: Jenius lived up to his name! He performed perfictly and got Full Marks and I am going to ask my ~~tea~~ teacher if I can take him to school and show them how briliant he is and how briliantly I have trained him. I'm the only person in the World who could have done it, I'm sure of that.

Jenius, it must be said, was not the only
one who had become a bit of a bighead, and
by the end of the first day back at school
everyone in the class was fed up with
hearing how clever both he and Judy were.
Before long Judy's teacher too had had
enough.

"Judy," she said. "You don't really expect
us to believe all this, do you?"

"Yes," said Judy. "It's true."

"Well, I'll tell you what. You bring this
amazing animal of yours into school and
then you can show us all these tricks that
you say he can do."

At once everyone wanted to get in on the
act and bring their pet to school.

"Oh, can I bring my rabbit?"

"...my gerbil?"

"...my hamster?"

"...my budgie?"

Until the teacher said "All right. We'll have a Pets' Day. You can each bring a pet in to school, provided you bring it in a cage or a box — we don't want anything too big, mind, no Shetland Ponies or Great Danes. Who knows, Judy, someone else may have a clever animal too."

Judy laughed. "Not as clever as Jenius," she said scornfully. "Not possibly. You just wait and see."

Like most people who keep diaries, Judy usually wrote in hers each evening. But as soon as she woke on the morning that had been chosen for Pets' Day, she opened it.

SEPTEMBER 11th: Today it is Pets' Day at school! Jenius will tryumph! * Watch this space! *

At breakfast time she could not contain herself. Till now she had said nothing to her parents — as she had sworn on July 23rd — of the progress of the Jenius, but she just knew she would not be able to resist describing the success that was to come before another hour had passed.

"What d'you think is happening today?" she said.

"You're going to be late for school," said her mother, "if you don't hurry up. And clean your shoes before you go. And take your anorak — it looks like rain."

"I'm taking Jenius to school," said Judy.

"Very nice, dear," said her mother. "Now, do you want an apple or a banana in your lunch box?"

"Apple," said Judy. "Dad, did you hear what I said?"

"I did," said her father from behind his morning paper. "Will he have to start in the Infants or is he clever enough to go straight into your class?"

"Oh Dad!" cried Judy. "Honestly, I really have trained him," and she rattled off a list of the things that Jenius could do.

"Judy," said her father. "You don't really expect us to believe all this, do you?"

"Yes," said Judy. "It's true."

Her father folded his newspaper.

"Now look here," he said. "Playing pretend games with your precious pet is one thing. But you mustn't confuse fantasy with truth."

There was hardly room to move in Judy's classroom that morning.

Everywhere there were hutches and cages and baskets and boxes containing pets. Only the Jenius was free, sitting perfectly still in front of Judy.

Judy's teacher saw what seemed to her a
rather odd-looking whitish guinea-pig,
with a crest of reddish hair sticking up
along its back, and said "Is this the genius
we've heard such a lot about?"

"Yes," said Judy proudly. "Shall I show
you what he can do?"

"All right," said her teacher. "Put him on
that big table in the middle of the room
where everyone can see him."

Ranged around the edges of the big table
were several pet-containers, a couple of
hamster-cages, a glass jar that held stick

insects, and a square basket that had one
open side barred with metal rods.

Fate decreed that Judy should put the
Jenius down quite near to this basket and
facing it, and though no one else could see
what was in it, he could. He looked
through the bars and saw a face, a
merciless face, with glowing yellow eyes
and a wide mouth filled with sharp white
teeth.

In fact the occupant of the basket was
only a half-grown kitten, but the sight of it

turned Jenius's legs to jelly and scrambled his brains. He was so frightened that he promptly Died For His Country, and there he lay, quite still and barely breathing. He could hear Judy's voice saying "Come!" and then, more loudly, "Jenius! Come!!" Then he heard a rising tide of noise which was the whole class first sniggering, then giggling, and finally laughing their heads off at clever Judy and her clever guinea-pig, about which she had boasted so loud and long. But he could not move a muscle.

"The great animal trainer!" someone said, and they laughed even more.

"Perhaps that will teach you a lesson,

Judy," said the teacher at last. "He doesn't seem to be quite the genius you told us he was. You mustn't confuse fantasy with truth."

"How did you get on, dear, your first day at school?" said Molly that evening.

"Need you ask?" growled Joe. "You were top of the class, weren't you, son? Got full marks for everything? Performed perfectly, eh?"

"No," said the Jenius in a small choked voice. "I didn't do anything."

"Well well well," said Joe. "The only guinea-pig in the world who can do all those tricks and he didn't do anything. I quite expected you to tell us you did something fantastic... Hopping like a rabbit perhaps. Or flying like a bird, I shouldn't be surprised."

Judy came in at that moment with a bunch of dandelions, to hear Joe and Molly making an awful racket. She thought they were yelling for food as usual but actually they were in fits of laughter.

"Flying! Oh Joe, you are a scream!" squealed Molly, and Joe, snorting with mirth, chuckled "Pride comes before a crash-landing!"

A few minutes later Judy's father, home from work, put his head in at the door of the shed.

"Well?" he said. "And did our genius perform all his amazing tricks?"

"No," said Judy. "He wouldn't do anything."

"Perhaps that will teach you a lesson, Judy," said her father.

Judy took a deep breath.

"Perhaps it has, Dad," she said. "But I wouldn't like you to think I was a liar."

"It's difficult for me not to think that," said her father, "when you tell me such fantastic things. For instance, that your guinea-pig can balance something on his nose and then throw it up and catch it. If he can do that, I'll eat my hat, I promise you."

"Watch," said Judy. She took a digestive out of her pocket and broke a piece off. She opened the door of Jenius' hutch.

"Come!" she said, and he came.

"Sit!" she said, and he sat.

Carefully she placed the fragment of biscuit on top of Jenius' snout.

"Trust!" she said, and he remained sitting bolt upright and stock-still for perhaps ten seconds, till Judy cried "Paid for!"

Up in the air sailed the bit of digestive and down it came again, straight into the

open mouth of the Jenius.

"*What* a good boy!" said Judy. "Now you can eat it up."

She turned to her father, who was bending down, hands on knees, watching in open-mouthed amazement, hat in hand. She took it from him.

"And you," she said, "can eat that."

PUFFIN BOOKS

Published by the Penguin Group
Penguin Books Ltd, 27 Wrights Lane, London W8 5TZ, England
Penguin Putnam Inc., 375 Hudson Street, New York, New York 10014, USA
Penguin Books Australia Ltd, Ringwood, Victoria, Australia
Penguin Books Canada Ltd, 10 Alcorn Avenue, Toronto, Ontario, Canada M4V 3B2
Penguin Books (NZ) Ltd, 182–190 Wairau Road, Auckland 10, New Zealand

Penguin Books Ltd, Registered Offices: Harmondsworth, Middlesex, England

First published by Victor Gollancz Ltd 1988
Published in Gollancz Children's Paperbacks 1990
Published in Puffin Books 1998
5 7 9 10 8 6 4

Text copyright © Dick King-Smith, 1988
Illustrations copyright © Peter Firmin, 1988
All rights reserved

Printed in Hong Kong by Wing King Tong

British Library Cataloguing in Publication Data
A CIP catalogue record for this book is available from the British Library

ISBN 0–140–38948–2

Other *Read It Yourself* titles